THE MAN OF STEEL

THE MOON BANDITS

WRITTEN BY
SCOTT SONNEBORN

ILLUSTRATED BY
MIKE CAVALLARO

SUPERMAN CREATED BY
JERRY SIEGEL AND
JOE SHUSTER

STONE ARCH BOOKS
a capstone imprint

PUBLISHED BY STONE ARCH BOOKS IN 2013
A CAPSTONE IMPRINT
1710 ROE CREST DRIVE
NORTH MANKATO, MN 56003
WWW.CAPSTONEPUB.COM

CATALOGING-IN-PUBLICATION DATA IS
AVAILABLE AT THE LIBRARY OF CONGRESS WEBSITE.

ISBN: 978-1-4342-4093-4 (LIBRARY BINDING)
ISBN: 978-1-4342-4223-5 (PAPERBACK)

SUMMARY: INTERGALACTIC ALIEN HIJACKERS HAVE STOLEN
EARTH'S MOON! SUPERMAN IS NOT ABOUT TO SIT BACK AND
WATCH HIS ADOPTED PLANET BE TORN APART BY TERRIBLE
TIDAL WAVES. THE MAN OF STEEL ZOOMS INTO SPACE TO
RECOVER THE STRAYING SATELLITE, BUT HE'S QUICKLY
OVERWHELMED. LEX LUTHOR, SUPERMAN'S ARCHENEMY,
OFFERS HIS HELP, BUT CAN SUPERMAN TRUST HIM?

ART DIRECTOR: BOB LENTZ AND BRANN GARVEY
DESIGNER: HILARY WACHOLZ

PRINTED IN THE UNITED STATES OF AMERICA IN
NORTH MANKATO, MINNESOTA.
092012   006933CGS13

TABLE OF CONTENTS

Years ago in a distant galaxy, the planet Krypton exploded. Its only survivor was a baby named Kal·El who escaped in a rocket ship. After landing on Earth, he was adopted by the Kents, a kind couple who named him Clark. The boy soon discovered he had extraordinary abilities fueled by the yellow sun of Earth. He chose to use these powers to help others, and so he became Superman - the guardian of his new home.

He is...

CHAPTER 1

THEY CAME FROM GALAXY X

Galaxy X was a dark place on the edge of the universe. It was so far from Earth that none of humanity's astronomers had any idea it even existed.

But the aliens who lived in Galaxy X knew plenty about Earth's solar system. The creatures from Galaxy X were called the Intellex. Twelve of them had made the trip from their home world to Venus.

The Intellex aliens looked at Venus's clouds of sulfuric acid and barren landscape.

"What makes this planet so perfect?" one Intellex asked. "It doesn't look so great to me."

"You're just not looking at it in the right way," insisted their foreman or leader, the Supreme Frank. "Use your imagination. This planet's 850-degree temperatures are perfect for a liquid metal ocean. Once we install one, we can charge a fortune for the luxury homes we'll build on its shores."

"And installing a liquid metal ocean will not be a problem for us," Frank reminded the eleven other Intellex in front of him. "Because we're the best crew of terraformers in the universe! There's no planet we can't alter or adapt, am I right?"

The other Intellex agreed — except for one.

"Yeah, but boss, this planet has no moon," the smallest one said. "Without the pull of a moon's gravity, the ocean we create won't have any tides or waves. That doesn't sound like much of an ocean to me."

"He's right," said another Intellex. "It takes forever to build a moon from scratch. If we don't open our development before the Junoans open theirs on the planet N'Cron . . ."

"I know, I know — we'll be out of business," said Frank. "But see, that's why this planet is so perfect. Because there's a moon we can use right next door."

Frank pointed to the green and blue planet next to Venus. A bright, white moon hovered near it.

"That's the moon we'll use," said Frank. "We'll steal it and bring it here into Venus's orbit."

"What will happen to that planet the moon is orbiting?" asked an Intellex.

"Without a moon to regulate its tides," replied Frank, "that planet's oceans will probably destroy most of the land." Frank shrugged. "But who cares? There is no highly evolved life like us there. Only a bunch of dumb animals live on the planet they call Earth."

* * *

Thirty-eight million miles away, the Man of Steel tumbled through a wall. **CRASH!** He landed hard inside an abandoned warehouse on the edge of Hob's Bay in Metropolis.

The man who had tossed Superman through the wall stood outside. He wore high-tech armor that increased his strength a thousand-fold. Which he proved by pulling the entire warehouse down on Superman!

RUMMMMMMMMMMMMMBLE!

The metal girders and wooden walls collapsed into a huge pile.

CRASH!

Superman was somewhere underneath, but nothing stirred. The only sound was the crunch of the armored man's metal boots as he walked over to the empty apartment building next door.

CRUNCH! The armored man sank his high-tech gloves into the side of the building.

As he began to pull, the Man of Steel exploded out of the wreckage of the warehouse. When he emerged, he saw the armored man tearing down the apartment building piece by piece.

"So, do you want to tell me why you're trying to wreck half of Hob's Bay on a beautiful morning like this?" asked Superman.

The armored man said nothing. Instead, he tore a wall off the apartment building.

WOOOOOOOOOSH! He threw it at the Man of Steel.

Superman frowned. "I'll take that as a 'no,'" he said.

ZIRRRRRT! ZIRRRRRT!

His heat vision blasted the wall into ashes.

I never thought I'd be glad that this part of Metropolis has gotten so run-down over the years, thought Superman. *But today it's a good thing, since it means there aren't any people around to get hurt.*

Superman lunged at the armored criminal.

KA-BLAM!

The man threw a punch that hit Superman across the face.

The punch was powerful enough to hurt the Man of Steel. But Superman managed to push the pain away and tackled the armored man to the ground with a loud **THUD!**

As they wrestled, Superman saw that the armor had no markings to identify it. But Superman's jaw was still sore.

That meant the man's armor packed a punch that was years ahead of the technology any army or government currently had. Superman knew only one person could have created armor as powerful as that.

Lex Luthor.

"I know you're working for Lex," Superman said to the armored man. "The only thing I don't know is why he sent you to tear down this neighborhood. But I don't need to know that in order to stop you once and for all."

WOOOOOOOOSH!

Superman ran at super-speed over to the fallen warehouse and grabbed an enormous steel girder. Then he dashed back over to the armored man.

The man was certainly powerful, but he was nowhere near as fast as Superman.

As the man threw punch after punch at him, Superman dodged the blows faster than the attacker could throw them. The super hero evaded the strikes, and then bent the steel girder in his hands.

CREEEEEEEEEAK!

The armored man wound up for one more big punch, but Superman ducked. The punch sailed over his head, putting the man momentarily off-balance. Superman used the opportunity to wrap the bent girder around his foe.

ZIRRRRRRRRRT!

ZIRRRRRRRRRRRRRRRT!

Superman sealed the girder in place with a blast of his heat vision.

The man struggled but could not break free.

The Man of Steel yanked the man's helmet off of his armor. A flurry of sparks and harsh sounds rang out.

Superman didn't recognize the man's face. But he did recognize Lex Luthor's voice shouting at the man through the helmet's radio.

"Report! Report!" Lex ordered. "Tell me what's going on!"

Superman smiled. "You've lost, Lex," he said.

Luthor just laughed.

HAHAHAHA!

"Why are you so confident, Superman?" Lex said. "How do you know I don't have an ace up my sleeve?"

"Lex —" began Superman. Then he stopped as a strange sight caught his eye. All the water in Hob's Bay — every last drop of it — suddenly went out with the tide!

Where did all the water go? thought Superman.

And then he saw it. A thousand foot tidal wave loomed over him. All the water in the bay had been pulled out to sea by the tide. And now, it was rushing back in one massive wave big enough to level an entire city.

Superman had never seen the tide do anything like that before.

But there was no time to wonder how it had happened. The massive wave was crashing into the docks and onto the empty streets in front of Superman.

ZAP! ZAP!

Superman blasted the water with his heat vision. Where he hit the wave, the water immediately turned to steam and faded harmlessly into the air. But there was simply too much water in the massive wave for him to vaporize it all.

KABOOOOOOOOOOM!

The wave crashed down on the street in front of him. Superman grabbed the armored man with both hands, lifting them both out of harm's way.

Flying above the surging wave, Superman saw a solid line of destruction.

RUMMMMMMBLE! Everything fell in the wave's path. Telephone poles, cars, and even buildings were carried inland by the water. They were all swept in the same direction by the wave, crashing and smashing together.

One large warehouse looked like it might be strong enough to resist the force of the massive tidal wave. But a moment later, it also crumpled beneath millions of tons of water.

THWOOOOOOOOOOOOM!

Nothing could withstand the wave's destructive force, but the Man of Steel didn't hesitate. He dropped the armored man on top of a high hill, then zoomed back toward the wave as it sliced through an abandoned building. Superman caught the top half of the building as it fell.

The building hit Superman with the force of a thousand tons of concrete and steel. Superman used every ounce of his strength to prevent the building from crushing him.

"Oomph!" grunted Superman. He dug his shoulder into the building and pushed with all his might. He began to lift the broken half upward. He set it down in the wave's path, using it as dam.

CRASH!

The building splintered as the wave exploded through it.

SPLOOSH!

The wave rammed into Superman, knocking him off his feet. Buried under millions of tons of water, the Man of Steel struggled to get back up.

Bit by bit, Superman fought his way up through the water. A few moments later, he burst into the sky.

The Man of Steel saw that the wave was heading out of Hob's Bay and into the busiest part of Metropolis!

And I've got no way to stop it! he realized.

Then, as quickly as it came, the wave receded. Just like any wave that hits the shore before being pulled back into the ocean, the giant tidal wave simply drained back into the harbor.

That was a close one, thought Superman.

Superman flew down to the armored man. He was still wrapped up like a gift with the metal girder.

"Lex!" shouted Superman into the man's helmet. "I don't know how you created that tidal wave —"

"That's because I didn't create it," Lex interrupted.

Over the radio, Superman could hear Lex's breathing and his heartbeat. He wasn't lying.

"So what on Earth did this, Lex?" demanded Superman.

"Nothing," came Lex's reply.

"Stop playing games," said Superman. "Obviously *something* did this."

"Yes, obviously," Lex replied coldly. "But as I said, it was nothing on Earth. Only one thing has that kind of power over the tides. And it's not on Earth. It's —"

Superman was already zooming up into the air before Lex could finish speaking. "The moon," he said to himself.

CHAPTER 2

TO THE MOON!

After racing to the secret location where he kept his space suit, Superman flew off toward the moon. *SWOOSH!*

Up, up, and up he soared — through the clouds and the atmosphere.

FWOOOOOOOM!

Superman punctured his way through the exosphere — the last barrier between Earth and outer space. Then he headed for the nearest source of light: the moon.

The moon doesn't generate its own light. It merely reflects the sun's light. But it was bright enough for the Man of Steel to see a dozen alien space robots on its surface.

The spacecraft looked like massive, robotic people, but each one was much larger than a human. Some of their parts looked like they were from construction vehicles. Two enormous pile drivers extended from the front of each robot.

I've never seen robots like those before, thought Superman. *They're definitely not from anywhere around here.*

Superman may not have recognized the robots. But he did recognize what they were doing. All twelve of the space robots had their massive pile drivers sunk deep into the lunar surface.

Anchored to the moon, the robots' engines roared as they slowly tugged the moon farther and farther away from Earth's orbit.

So far, they'd only moved the moon a few miles, which was almost nothing compared to the distance between the moon and Earth. But even that comparably small shift had caused massive tidal waves all over the planet.

Lex was right about the moon, thought the Man of Steel. *When it comes to science and math, Lex always knows the right answer.*

In addition to his accomplishments as a genetic engineer, microbiologist, and chemist, Lex Luthor was also a gifted astrophysicist.

How can one man be right about so many things, Superman thought, *yet be so wrong about others?*

There would be time to figure that out later. At the moment, Superman had bigger concerns, like the twelve gigantic robots that were stealing Earth's moon.

Superman aimed at the nearest one. *SWOOOOOOOSH!*

He zoomed in and pulled at one of the giant pile drivers anchoring the robot to the moon. He put every muscle into it and yanked it out! *FWOOOOOOOOOM!*

"Hey, stop that!" a voice boomed from the robot. "What do you think you're doing? This is an Intellex work site! Authorized personnel only!"

SLICK!

The freed pile driver slithered out of Superman's grip. Then it slammed him down and pinned him to the ground with a **THUD!**

The Man of Steel struggled with all his strength, but he could not break free.

"Hey, boss!" the robot's voice boomed again. "It looks like some kind of animal has wandered into the work site."

"Well, get rid of it," replied the Supreme Frank. "We're on a tight schedule here!"

"Got it, boss," boomed the voice from the first robot. **CLANK!** Its pile driver arm smacked Superman like a golf club, sending him flying into a crater more than a mile away.

THUMP! Superman landed hard on the ground.

That didn't go very well, he thought. *I've never heard of these Intellex before. I need to know what I'm up against — let's see what kind of aliens they are.*

The Man of Steel used his X-ray vision to look inside one of the robots, searching for the alien crew.

Superman was shocked by what he saw, or rather, by what he didn't see. There was no crew inside the robots at all! Every inch of the robot was crammed full of wires and pipes. Aside from the weird sponge-like objects in their domes, they looked completely robotic.

As Superman evaluated the robot's interior, it started to look less and less like the inside of a robot, and more like veins and organs inside a human's body.

There are no aliens in any of these robots! They must be remote controlled, thought Superman. He let out a sigh of relief. *Which means I don't have to worry about hurting anyone inside them.*

Superman leaped up from the crater and flew toward the nearest robot. With his fists out in front of him, he rocketed full-speed into the spacecraft.

KA-CHING!

Superman hit the robot with enough force to crush an oil tanker. The spacecraft shuddered and let out a metallic moan.

"That's it!" boomed the Supreme Frank's voice from his robot. "We can't have any dumb animals interfering with our work! Everybody, take a five minute break and get rid of this intruder!"

Suddenly, all the robots retracted their pile drivers from the moon and rushed toward Superman. The first robot slammed into him.

SLASH!

Its metal pile drivers raked Superman across the chest and knocked him down.

BOOM! A cloud of dust flew up as Superman tumbled onto the moon's surface. He saw another pile driver coming and quickly rolled away.

WHAM! The pile driver slammed into the rock next to him, exploding it into a thousand fragments.

As the other Intellex fought Superman, Frank the foreman noticed that the moon was slowly drifting back toward its normal orbit of Earth.

"When we stop tugging, Earth's gravity starts to pull the moon back into place!" cried Frank. "All the work we've done has been wasted! Hurry up and get rid of that animal already, or we'll all be stuck doing mandatory overtime!"

Several long sighs came from the Intellex robots' speakers. Then they surged against Superman, attempting to overwhelm him.

He fought hard against the massive robots. He was as strong as any of them. But together, the Intellex robots were powerful enough to move the moon. When they worked as a team, they were more than a match for even the Man of Steel.

BAM! BAM!

BAMMMMMMMMMMM!

They pounded Superman with their massive pile drivers. He blocked some of the blows, but others hit him hard enough to send him plummeting back toward Earth.

VRRRROOOMM!

Superman tumbled down through the atmosphere. He was completely out of control and unable to stop.

ZOOOOOOOOOOM!

As he fell faster and faster, the heat grew more and more intense.

WOOOOOOOSH!

Superman's space suit glowed like a marshmallow in a campfire as its edges began to char. The intense heat began to make Superman fear for his life.

Just before his suit burst into flame, Superman caught himself in the air and stopped falling. His spacesuit cooled. He let out a quick sigh of relief.

Until he looked down. Below him, a mile-high tidal wave threatened to swamp Metropolis!

The wave was easily ten times bigger than the one that had hit Hob's Bay. One look at the killer wave, and Superman knew he had to act fast.

If this one hits Metropolis, he realized, *it will wipe out the whole city!*

CHAPTER 3

TIDAL FORCES

Superman zoomed down toward Metropolis. Still several miles out to sea, the giant wave cast an eerie shadow over the entire city.

SWOOOOOOSH! Superman smashed into the surging tide with his fists. The massive wave simply flipped him and tossed him up in the air.

Superman found himself involuntarily surfing on top of the thousand-foot wave. It was carrying him straight toward Metropolis.

I've got to stop this thing now! he thought.

Superman flew back up into the air and rocketed ahead of the wave. Then he dived straight down into the ocean. *SPLOOSH!*

As soon as he hit the water, he turned and swam in a circle. He raced around and around, moving faster and faster. Superman spun the water so quickly that it formed a whirlpool.

SPLASH!

The front edge of the wave washed over Superman and hit the swirling whirlpool.

GURGLE!

The whirlpool's vortex swallowed the bottom of the wave and then pulled the rest down after it.

To Superman, it looked as if a watery vacuum cleaner was sucking the entire wave down.

Seconds later, the mighty wave disappeared completely.

Superman stopped swimming. The whirlpool faded away. The waters of Hob's Bay were calm once again.

I've saved the city, thought Superman, *for now. But if those Intellex move the moon even farther away, these waves will just get worse!*

No other super heroes would be able to help him fight the aliens. The movement of the moon was affecting every ocean on the entire planet. That meant every coastal city was at risk of being swamped by a tidal wave.

Green Lantern, the Flash, even Batman would be too busy protecting their own cities to help the Man of Steel save Metropolis.

As he flew high over Metropolis, Superman grew worried. *But if I fight the Intellex on the moon,* he thought, *then who will protect my city?*

Suddenly, a voice boomed out through the radio in his space suit. "SUPERMAN!" it said.

Superman recognized the voice immediately. "Lex!" he replied. "How did you figure out the frequency of my space suit's radio?"

Lex chuckled. "The parts used for the radio in your suit were invented by LexCorp," he said.

Superman was pretty sure Lex was smiling as he spoke. "I see," he said. "So what do you want?"

"We need to talk," Lex said. "Meet me at the LexCorp balcony."

Superman looked down. Using his super-vision, he saw Lex Luthor standing on a balcony atop his corporate tower in midtown Metropolis.

It doesn't look like a trap, Superman thought. *But I better be on my guard anyway.*

THUMP!

Superman landed next to Lex. "What is it now, Lex?" asked the Man of Steel. "I'm a little busy saving the planet — including Metropolis."

"This is my city, too," said Lex.

"That's why I called you down here," Lex explained. "I've seen what you're up against on the moon. And to answer your next question before you even ask it, LexCorp has the most advanced telescopes on the planet. That's how I saw you."

Superman narrowed his eyes. "Get to the point, Lex," he said impatiently.

"Go back up there and keep our moon where it belongs," Lex continued. "My men will divert any tidal waves that get close to Metropolis. They've got the armor to get the job done — I think I proved that to you in Hob's Bay."

Superman nodded. The armored man he fought in Hob's Bay was incredibly strong. If Lex had more men in his service like him, they should be able to keep Metropolis dry and safe.

Still, there was one question nagging at Superman. "Why would you help me?" he asked.

"Like I said, this is my city," replied Lex. "Even more than it is yours, if you think about it. After all, I was born on this planet, and I've lived here longer."

Superman didn't know if he could trust Luthor. In fact, he knew that he probably shouldn't. But if he didn't get back to the moon and find a way to stop the Intellex, the waves threatening Metropolis would just get bigger and bigger.

Suddenly, everything went dark. It was like someone had switched off the lights, turning day to night. Superman looked up and saw what had happened. It was an eclipse. The Intellex had dragged the moon so far that it was blocking the sun!

It's going to take everything I've got to keep the moon where it belongs, thought Superman. *I don't have a choice. I have to trust Lex.*

"You're running out of time, Superman," cried Lex. "Now get back up there and save my city!"

The twelve Intellex robots were anchored to the moon. **WHIR-WHIR-WHIR!** Their engines roared as they pulled the moon farther out into space.

They were so busy working that they didn't even notice Superman fly up toward them. He ducked down in a crater to hide and observe.

Superman saw the Supreme Frank. *I'm only going to get one shot at this,* he thought. Cautiously, he snuck toward the Intellex.

THWOK! Frank smacked Superman across the legs with both of its pincer-shaped pile drivers.

THUMP! The Man of Steel tumbled back down into the crater.

"Did you really think you could surprise us?" asked Frank. "My radar picked you up as soon as you left your planet's atmosphere. I've been in this business too long to let the same animal wander into my work site twice in one Earth day!"

Superman got back to his feet. "It's bad enough that you're wrecking my planet," he said. "But do you really have to insult me while you do it? I was already going to destroy your robots, but now I'm going to enjoy it!"

WHOOOOOOOOOOOOOOSH!

In a blur, the Man of Steel flew at the Intellex robots. The lumbering robots were ten times larger than him and just as strong, but Superman was much faster!

SHOOOOOOM! He zipped in between them and grabbed hold of Frank's pincers. Holding tight, Superman zoomed away with Frank as fast he could. By the time the other Intellex robots had pulled their pincers free from the moon, Superman and Frank were gone.

As Superman towed the Supreme Frank farther and farther away from the moon, the robot slashed at the Man of Steel with its pile drivers.

SLASH!

SLASH!

Superman hit back — hard.

The blows dented the robot's hull but didn't seem to do any real damage.

My punches barely dent the robot's surface, thought Superman. Then he smiled. *Well, this hull may be thick, but it sure looks like there's plenty of delicate equipment inside!*

Superman dug his fingers into the robot.

CLUNK!

Then he shook as hard as he could.

SHUKA-SHUKA-SKUKA.

"Stop!" cried Frank.

The robot's pincers slashed and jabbed at Superman with its pile drivers. Superman ignored the blows and kept shaking the robot as violently as he could.

WHIR-WHIR-WHIR-WHIR!

Frank's mammoth engines began to slow. Then the engine shut down with a deafening **CLANK!**

Superman stopped shaking the robot for a moment. The vessel hung limply in Superman's hands.

Suddenly, an unearthly roar came from the robot. "Owwwwwwww!" the voice said. "That really hurt!"

Superman double-checked with his X-ray vision. There was no one inside the robot. "How could I have hurt you?" asked Superman. "There isn't anyone inside the robot."

"Inside?" howled the Supreme Frank. "Inside what! I'm right here in your hands, you big, dumb, dirty animal!"

Superman's eyes went wide.

"These robots aren't controlled by aliens," he said. "They *are* the aliens. The robots are alive!"

CHAPTER 4

IT'S ALIVE!

Superman frowned. "So those spongey things on your bodies," he said, "are your brains?!"

"Of course!" roared the Supreme Frank as he lay motionless in Superman's grip. "I guess I shouldn't be surprised you didn't know. Animals like you are nowhere near as smart as living machines like us."

Superman sighed. "I'm just glad I didn't smash any of you to pieces when I thought you were just remote controlled robots," he said.

"Is that what you thought we were?" growled Frank. "You really are a dumb animal, you know that? Now let me go so I can get back to work."

Superman frowned. "If you're really so much smarter than I am," he said, "then you must know that taking the moon out of its orbit will damage the Earth."

"I sure do," said Frank. He gestured with his pile driver arms while he talked. "Look, it's nothing personal, it's just business. I know enough about your planet to know you can understand that. What we're doing to your moon is no different than when humans build a dam that blocks a river that some fish depended on. If there's money to be made, you don't worry about the damage to a handful of lesser life forms. Neither do we."

"Even if some people on Earth do that," Superman said, "it doesn't mean you should do the same thing to a whole planet. Two wrongs don't make a right!"

"I didn't say it was wrong," replied Frank. "I think it's totally the right thing to do! Sure, your planet will suffer when we move this moon. In fact, it'll probably get completely destroyed. But my crew and I will make a fortune! You can't even comprehend how much money is on the line here. Trust me, it's too much money to let some lesser life-forms like you interfere."

"We aren't lesser life-forms," Superman said through clenched teeth.

"You definitely are," argued Frank. "Just look how you treat your machines! You treat them even worse than you treat fish. You act like you own them."

"Besides," Frank continued, "you tell your cars to drive you wherever you want with no concern for their feelings at all!"

"But cars don't have feelings!" Superman said. "They're just machines!"

"Just machines?!" howled the insulted Frank. "I'm a machine, and believe me, I have feelings. For example, right now I feel very happy to see that the rest of my crew has finally caught up to us!"

SLASH! SLASH! SLASH!

The other Intellex slashed at Superman with their enormous pile drivers.

"Put this pest down," ordered Frank. "We need to get back to work and MOVE THIS MOON!"

"Wait!" Superman shouted as he fought off the other Intellex.

"You're putting an entire planet of people in danger!" Superman said. "You've got to listen to me!" But he knew it was useless.

We're just too different, Superman realized. *To the Intellex, it doesn't matter what happens to everyone on Earth as long as they get what they want.*

It was clear to Superman that there was only one way to stop the Intellex. He had to fight them — and win. Unfortunately, it was not at all clear how Superman would be able to do that.

BAM!

WHAM!

Superman knocked back the first robot that attacked him. And the second. But more Intellex just zoomed right at him.

Superman grabbed the nearest one and started to shake it. But the others slashed and stabbed at him with their pile drivers, pulling him off before he could disable its engines.

They're not going to let me battle them one by one, thought Superman. *I've got to find a way to shake them all at once!*

But it was hard to form a plan while six Intellex were pounding him with their pile drivers. **SLAM! SLAM! SLAM!**

A blow struck Superman on the back of his head. **CLUNK!**

Superman's body went limp. He drifted off into space.

"Finally," said the Supreme Frank. "That animal was getting to be a real work site hazard."

"Is it dead?" asked a Intellex.

"Who can tell?" replied Frank. "It is such a strange life-form. I have no idea how it even works."

SPUTTER! SPUTTER! Frank tried to fly back toward the moon, but couldn't. His coworkers stared at him in confusion. When he spoke, he almost sounded embarrassed. "Say, um," he said quietly, "do any of you happen to have a spare internal driver?"

The Intellex searched themselves. "I have one extra," one Intellex said.

"One's enough," said Frank. "Now you all get back to work while I install this driver. We're way behind schedule!"

The Intellex buried their pincer-like pile drivers back into the moon's surface.

SHLUNK! SHLUNK! SHLUNK!

"Pull!" ordered the Supreme Frank.

WHIR-SPUTTER-WHIR! The alien robots strained their engines. The moon moved slowly.

"Good work," declared the Supreme Frank. He began to install his replacement part as he spoke. "Now let's move this moon to Venus!"

Above them, Superman drifted in space, his body completely still. No part of him was moving. Except his mouth — which suddenly smiled!

Superman opened his eyes. He had only been pretending to be knocked out.

I didn't think they'd be able to tell if I was playing possum or not, thought Superman. *Well it sure looks like I was right!*

With the Intellex locked into the moon, Superman flew down toward them. Zooming as fast as he could, he reached them before they could pull their pincers free to defend themselves. But Superman wasn't aiming for the Intellex. Instead, he smashed into the moon itself.

KA-POW!

The moon shook from the impact. But Superman didn't stop there. **SLAM! WHAM! BAM!** He pounded the moon's surface as hard as he could. **RUMMMBLE!** A massive moon-quake rippled out from the crater he'd created.

VROOM-WOOM-WOOM-WOOM!

The quake's vibrations rumbled up through the Intellex's pile drivers that connected them to the moon.

RUDDA-RUDDA-RUDDA! The moon-quake shook the Intellex harder than anything Superman had thrown at them before. **SPUTTER! SPUTTER! SPUTTER!** One by one, their engines shut down. All the Intellex were stuck to the moon by their pile drivers!

All except Frank. He had been busy using his pole-arms to replace his internal driver. "WHAT HAVE YOU DONE?!" Frank roared.

SMACK! Frank tackled Superman with his pincer arms.

"You knocked out my whole crew!" Frank shouted. He squeezed Superman between his powerful pincers. "Now there's no way I can build my development before my competition can build theirs! This job is ruined!"

Holding Superman tight, Frank pulled him off the moon. As the moon began drifting back into its proper place, Frank began to crush the Man of Steel between his pile drivers.

"You just cost me more money than your primitive meat-brain can even compute," the Supreme Frank roared. "So now I'm going to make YOU pay!"

BAMMMMMMMMM!

BAMMMMMMMMM!

Superman slammed back with his fists but couldn't break loose from Frank's iron grip. The two tumbled toward Earth.

As they dropped through the atmosphere, Superman looked down. Below him, he saw Metropolis — and another giant wave about to crash into it!

Frank squeezed tighter. Superman couldn't break free. "Lex!" Superman shouted over his space suit's radio. "I've stopped the Intellex from moving the moon. But there's one last wave heading toward Metropolis!"

KABLAM! Frank whacked Superman with one of his massive pile drivers as they continued to fall.

"I see you're still a little too busy to take care of it," replied Lex over the radio. "My men have already put in place a barrier that will deflect the wave in a more productive direction."

"Wait," Superman said to Luthor as he blasted back at Frank with his heat vision. "What do you mean 'a more productive direction'?"

"Well, in business one often has to make decisions that help some people but also hurt others," said Luthor.

"Business?" asked Superman. "What are you talking about? We had a deal, Lex!"

"Absolutely," agreed Luthor. "And the deal was that my men would divert any wave that approached the city. And they will. Right toward Hob's Bay!"

CHAPTER 5

BUSINESS AS USUAL

"But the people there will be swamped!" Superman shouted. "There aren't many people living in Hob's Bay, but there are still some!"

THWACK!

Frank punched at Superman as the two plummeted down together through the clouds.

"Trust me, this is better for Metropolis," replied Luthor over the space suit's radio.

"With the poor people of Hob's Bay gone," Luthor explained, "Metropolis won't have to waste money on taking care of them. Everyone else will benefit from their deaths after I build a new development over the ruins of Hob's Bay."

Superman struggled against Frank's grip. "You're insane!" Superman yelled.

"You interrupted my first attempt to destroy Hob's Bay," said Luthor, "when you stopped my armored man this morning. This tidal wave is merely an opportunity to make up for the profits that you cost me."

"You know I'm going to stop you, Lex," Superman said.

KRACKA-BAM!

Frank struck Superman again as they plunged toward Metropolis.

"It looks to me like you have your hands full at the moment," said Luthor. "But it doesn't matter. It's already too late. The little whirlpool trick you used to stop that other tidal wave won't work this time. This wave is much larger."

KA·CHUNK! Frank slammed Superman with a pile driver.

ZAP! Superman blasted back with his heat vision.

"But you'll try to stop it anyway," continued Lex, "and seeing you try — and fail — will convince the people of Metropolis that you're to blame for the destruction of Hob's Bay. Telling people I'm responsible will just sound to them like a guilty man trying to shift the blame."

Superman was surprised by Lex. This sinister plan was too sick and twisted — even for Lex Luthor. "You said this was your city!" Superman said.

"Yes," agreed Luthor. "Mine to do with as I please!"

HAHAHAHAHA! Lex's laugh made Superman realize there was no way he was going to convince Luthor he was wrong. Lex just saw things too differently. He couldn't see past his own desires and needs.

He's just like the Intellex, Superman realized. *Completely and totally selfish.*

KA-CLANG!

Superman pounded on Frank's metal hull, finally breaking loose from the Intellex's grip.

"I don't know who you were just talking to," said Frank as he swung at Superman. "But I hope you enjoyed the conversation — because it's going to be your last!"

BAM! Frank hit Superman so hard he tumbled over in the air. Facing down, Superman saw the barrier Lex's armored men had created in the ocean in front of Metropolis. The towering wave would hit it any moment.

WHAM! WHAM! WHAM!

Frank pummeled Superman again and again.

How am I going to cut that wave down to size AND deal with him? Superman wondered.

And then suddenly, he realized how. Superman zoomed away from Frank.

"Get back here!" shouted Frank as he raced after him.

SPLOOOOOOOOOOOOSH! Superman dived into the ocean between the giant wave and the barrier Lex's armored men had created.

BWA-SPLASH!

Frank hit the water right after him. Superman ripped through the water like a torpedo. Frank chased him straight down to the ocean floor.

When Superman hit the bottom, he kept going. He burrowed a tunnel under the ocean that was too small for the gigantic Frank.

"You think you can hide in there?" howled Frank.

FWOOM! FWOOM! FWOOM!

Frank used his pile drivers to dig a trench so that he could follow Superman. As Superman burrowed deeper, so did Frank.

FWOOM! FWOOM! FWOOM!

Chasing Superman, Frank had dug a massive trench almost half a mile deep when the tidal wave finally reached it. The wave was so huge that when it hit the bottom of the trench, it shook the seafloor with a colossal **RUMBLE!**

Inside the trench, Frank could not escape the shaking. **WHIR-WHIR-WHIR-WHIR!** His engine moaned with effort. Superman saw the sea-quake shake Frank so hard that all of his systems failed.

SPUTTER! SPUTTER!

Frank shut down completely.

Until he got some replacement parts, Frank was down for the count.

The sea-quake rippled out from the trench. **RUMMMBLE!** It shook and shattered the support beams holding up the barrier that Lex's men had created.

SPLOOSH!

The barrier fell into pieces, dumping the men into the water.

ZAP!

Their high-tech armor shorted out, leaving the technology useless.

The last of the wave poured into the trench. From above the ocean, it looked as if the entire wave had suddenly dropped under the water and disappeared. The surface of the ocean was now completely calm.

Standing on the balcony of his corporate tower, Lex Luthor saw only the smallest ripple of water lap up against the shores of Metropolis. Hob's Bay and the rest of the city were safe!

Suddenly, **SPLOOOOOOSH!** Water poured down over Luthor, drenching him. Soaked, Luthor looked up to see Superman holding the massive Frank. The unconscious alien was dripping wet.

Superman smiled. "Oops," he said. "I guess he still had a little ocean water in him. You don't mind if I leave him here until S.T.A.R. Labs picks him up, do you?"

Without waiting for a reply, Superman dropped the helpless Frank on top of Lex's tower.

CRUNCH!

Frank smashed into the roof, breaking dozens of windows.

"Ouch!" Frank cried out, unable to move.

"Oops," Superman said to Frank. "Clumsy me."

Superman turned to face Lex again. "Sorry about that," he said. "But hey, I guess now you can take all that money you were going to spend building a development on top of Hob's Bay and use it to fix up your tower instead."

Lex could only fume.

"Just remember," Superman said to both Luthor and the incapacitated alien. "The next time either of you do something that threatens my city, I won't be so forgiving."

And with that, Superman flew off over the still, shining waters of Hob's Bay.

LEX LUTHOR

Real Name:
Lex Luthor

Occupation:
Mastermind

Base:
Metropolis

Height:
6 feet 2 inches

Weight:
210 lbs.

Eyes:
Green

Hair:
None

Lex Luthor is one of the richest and most powerful people in all of Metropolis. He's known as a successful businessman to most, but Superman knows Luthor's dirty little secret: most of his wealth is ill-gotten, and behind the scenes he is a criminal mastermind.

- Superman has stopped many of Luthor's sinister schemes, but Lex is always careful to avoid getting caught red-handed by using Earth's laws to his advantage.

- Lex wants to destroy Superman to strengthen his grip on Metropolis, but the Man of Steel is immune to Luthor's influence.

- While lacking superpowers of his own, Lex has developed several incredible electronic inventions, including his trademark armored battlesuit that puts his powers on par with the Man of Steel's.

BIOGRAPHIES

SCOTT SONNEBORN has written many books, one circus (for Ringling Bros. Barnum & Bailey), and a bunch of TV shows. He's been nominated for one Emmy and spent three very cool years working at DC Comics. He lives in Los Angeles with his wife and their two sons.

MIKE CAVALLARO is originally from New Jersey, where he attended the Joe Kubert School of Cartoon and Graphic Art, and has worked in comics and animation since the early 1990's. Mike's comics include "Parade (with fireworks)", a Will Eisner Comics Industry Award-nominee, "The Life and Times of Savior 28", written by J.M. DeMatteis, and "Foiled", written by Jane Yolen. Mike is a member of the National Cartoonists Society and lives in Brooklyn, NY.

GLOSSARY

astrophysicist (as-troh-FIZ-uh-sist)—someone who studies the physical and chemical properties, origin, and evolution of the stars and other celestial bodies

barren (BA-ruhn)—if land is barren, crops cannot be grown on it

crater (KRAY-tur)—a large hole in the ground caused by something like a bomb or meteorite

eclipse (i-KLIPS)—the partial or complete blocking of the light of one star or planet by another

evolved (i-VOLVD)—changed slowly, sometimes over many years

girder (GUR-dur)—a large, heavy beam made of steel or concrete that is used in construction

harbor (HAR-bur)—a place where ships shelter or unload their cargo

hazard (HAZ-urd)—a danger or risk

tidal force (TYE-duhl FORSS)—on Earth, the gravitational pull by the moon that raises the tides within the gravitational field. Tides are dependent on the varying distance between the bodies.

DISCUSSION QUESTIONS

1. Who was more evil in this story — the alien Intellex, or Lex Luthor? Explain your answer.

2. Do you think alien life exists somewhere in our universe? Why or why not?

3. This book has ten illustrations. Which one is your favorite? Why?

WRITING PROMPTS

1. Superman's space suit lets him communicate with others in the vacuum of space. Design an underwater suit for Superman. What does it look like? What features and gadgets does it have? Write about it, then draw a picture of it.

2. From Superman's perspective, write a short letter to the Intellex aliens trying to convince them to leave Earth's moon where it is.

3. The Intellex are an alien race of robots. Design your own alien robot! Write a few paragraphs about your character, then draw a picture of it.